The Awakening

First published 2013 by
A & C Black, an imprint of Bloomsbury Publishing Plc
50 Bedford Square, London, WC1B 3DP

www.acblack.com
www.bloomsbury.com

Copyright © 2013 A & C Black
Text copyright © 2013 Paul Mason
Illustrations copyright © 2013 Sean Longcroft

ISBN 978-1-4081-8067-9

A CIP catalogue for this book is available from the British Library.

Printed and bound by CPI Group (UK) Ltd, Croydon CR0 4YY

1 3 5 7 9 10 8 6 4 2

MIX
Paper from
responsible sources
FSC
www.fsc.org   FSC® C020471

The Awakening

PAUL MASON

Illustrated by
Sean Longcroft

A & C BLACK
AN IMPRINT OF BLOOMSBURY
LONDON NEW DELHI NEW YORK SYDNEY

For Mia and Miles

Contents

Chapter One

Danger!

Zaf stood at the edge of the deep split in the ground and stared in shock at the meter in his hands. The needle was jammed in the red zone. Jammed in the part of the dial that said 'Danger' in big, red writing.

He tapped the glass a couple of times to make sure it wasn't stuck. The needle didn't budge. This was strange, really strange, and Mr Arturi was still back at the van. Maybe they shouldn't have gone on ahead without him.

Zaf called to the others further down the track. 'Guys, you'd better come take a look at this.' He pointed to the crack in the ground.

'What's up?' Tara was the first over. April and Ian weren't far behind.

'This reading I'm getting. We're nowhere near the hot spot and the machine's going crazy. It must be broken, right?'

'That's odd.' Tara looked at Zaf's meter. She pulled her backpack off her shoulder and fished out her own meter. April and Ian did the same.

The readers crackled into life. One by one the needles hit the top of the dial. The red zone.

'I don't think your machine's broken,' Tara said slowly.

Now there was a rumbling from deep inside the ground.

April's eyes widened. 'Guys, I think we should…'

'RUN!' shouted Ian. He pulled at Tara and Zaf, dragging the team away from the hole.

Too little, too late.

BLAM! An explosion blasted out of the ground like a bomb going off. Dirt and rocks burst high into the air. Water erupted from the hole.

The four were blown off their feet, picked up and thrown to the ground like toys. Dirt and hot water rained down on them, a fountain of sludge.

As suddenly as it had started, it stopped.

Now a cloud of thick, yellow gas began to spill out

THE FOUR WERE THROWN TO THE GROUND LIKE **TOYS**...

of the hole. A blanket of smoke slowly wrapped itself around the helpless shapes lying on the ground. The four friends gasped for breath, choking, as the fog started to seep into their lungs.

***

Ian was the first to come around.

Everything was a blur. There was a mask strapped to his face, and his throat burned. His hands were wrapped in white bandages. He ached all over.

He tried to sit up, but quickly gave up and sank back onto the bed. *This must be hospital*, he thought. *Great. Just great. Some science trip* that *turned out to be.*

The monitor he was hooked up to started to beep.

Ian's eyes cleared a little and he was able to prop himself up on his elbows. The others were in the room, all asleep, or unconscious. Like him, they had bandages. And probably felt like they'd just gone twelve rounds.

The door to the room swung open and a doctor rushed over to Ian's bed, followed by Mr Arturi. He looked sick with worry.

The doctor took Ian's mask off and started looking into his eyes with one of those little pen lights. 'How do you feel?' she asked.

Silly question, thought Ian but he just said 'OK, I guess.'

The others began to stir now and open their eyes. The doctor quickly checked each of them in turn. Mr Arturi let out a big sigh, as if he had been holding his breath this whole time. 'Thank goodness, thank goodness,' was all he could say, over and over.

'You're certainly lucky,' the doctor added.

'What happened?' groaned Tara. 'I remember a blast, and then nothing.'

'It was a hydro-thermal eruption. A big one. Knocked all of you right out.' Mr Arturi shook his head. 'I should never have gone back to the van for more equipment. I should have been there.'

'A thermo-hydro what?' mumbled Ian.

'Hydro-thermal,' whispered Zaf, propping himself up slowly. 'A combination of heat and water. From deep below the earth's crust.'

Mr Arturi nodded. 'It must have been building up.' He shook his head. 'I had no idea this would happen, there were no warnings. I'm so sorry.'

'Hey, Mr Arturi.' April smiled weakly. 'It wasn't your fault.'

Mr Arturi took her hand. 'Am I glad to see that smile of yours, April.' He turned to the others. 'I've called all your parents, they're driving up. They'll be here soon.'

'Just one question,' said Ian with a grin. 'Does this mean we get to miss school?'

Chapter Two

Fire

Back at school, word quickly got round about the explosion, and how Mr Arturi had carried the four friends to the van to rescue them. The rest of the class stared at the bandages the four were still wearing, the burn marks on their arms. Everyone wanted to know the story.

'Why don't you take a photograph, it'll last longer,' Ian told a boy sitting at their table in the dining hall.

'Just ignore him,' April sighed, rolling her eyes. 'Ian's had a blow to the head, poor child.'

Ian laughed. 'I'm only kidding.'

Tara picked up her tray. 'Don't forget, you two,

we've got to meet Mr Arturi after school to go over the readings from the site – Zaf says the data from the meters is off the chart.'

'I'll be there,' said April.

'No can do,' said Ian. 'Track practice. It's only a week before the big meet and I need to get in shape. Sorry, Miss,' he teased.

***

Ian was pounding the track on his own, getting in a few extra laps. He needn't have worried that the explosion had taken it out of him. He was doing well. In fact he was doing better than 'well': he was cruising. *This feels good*, he said to himself, checking his watch as he crossed the lap marker.

Ian pushed himself even harder. His legs and arms were pumping, his feet flying down the track. He became just a blur. But he still felt like he had more to give. He picked up the pace. There was an energy flowing round his body. Something new. The soles of his feet felt like they were burning up the track. It was getting hot. Really hot.

Ian glanced down at his legs. Fire!

IAN WAS **BURNING UP** THE **TRACK**!

With a scream of terror he fell over and started slapping at his feet. They were on fire! Fire! Orange flames were all over his skin. Ian rolled around, trying to put the fire out.

Then all of a sudden, the flames were gone. Just like that.

Panting, Ian ripped off his smoking shoes and socks and threw them away. The skin underneath was untouched. Not even reddened. Ian rubbed his head in amazement.

'Mr Arturi has just *got* to see this,' he said out loud.

Chapter Three

Water

While things were heating up on the track, April had decided to cool off at the beach. The meeting with Mr Arturi had been really long, and all those numbers had given her a serious headache.

She dumped her stuff in her room, quickly slipped into her costume, and grabbed a towel. She ran through the kitchen, waving at Mum. 'I'll be back for dinner!' she yelled.

The beach was pretty much empty when April got down there. Just a few families packing up further down the bay. It was still hot even though the sun was going down, and April gasped as she stepped into the cool water. She let the water reach just above her knees, then she dived in. The sea sent a ripple over her skin and she burst to the surface with a smile on her face.

April swum further out to sea, away from the beach. Soon she couldn't touch the sand. She dropped down beneath the surface and somersaulted lazily in the water. She twisted and turned like a fish. April loved being in the ocean. It felt like home.

It was then she noticed the fin.

At first she thought it was a wave. But it turned round, and headed straight for her. Cutting through the water like a razor. A cold, grey razor.

Shark!

The fin sliced lower into the water now, and vanished into the dark.

April knew she should to stay still. She wanted not to panic, not to draw attention to herself. But she freaked. She kicked out with her legs. *I have to get to the beach!* She clawed at the water with her hands, her arms slapping and splashing. There was no way she could outswim a shark.

Then it happened. Not the feeling of jagged teeth grabbing hold of her skin - but something else.

She vanished.

April had totally disappeared. Her arms, her legs, her entire body. She couldn't see herself at all. Just an empty swimsuit. One moment her legs and arms were churning up the water. Then they were gone. Just gone.

I must be dead, April thought in a panic. *The shark must have got me. This is just a weird out-of-body death thing*. But she felt alive. In fact she felt more alive than ever before. She stopped swimming and lifted her arm out of the water. It was the shape of her arm, but it was like it was made of water. It was the same colour as the sea. It *was* the sea. Her other arm too. What was going on?

'THIS IS JUST A WEIRD **OUT-OF-BODY** DEATH THING!'

Then something even stranger: the shark barrelled past her, tail carving through the water. Right next to her body, so she could even feel its skin, see its shadow, feel the might of its tail. She yelped.

But the shark had gone right past her. How could it have missed her? *Because I'm made of water*, April thought, heart pounding.

The shark gave up. April saw its fin break the water's surface and then it headed back out to sea, wondering how it had lost its prey.

April raced back to the shore - except it felt more like she flowed there. As she stepped onto the sand and walked out of the water, her body changed back in front of her eyes, from water into flesh. She looked around the beach to see if anyone else might have seen, but she was alone.

A grin broke out on her face from ear to ear. She didn't know what was going on, but whatever it was, it felt good.

April grabbed her towel and dried off. She was late for dinner. She wouldn't tell Mum and Dad why, though. Not until she had figured out what was going on.

Chapter Four

Hallucination

'You're not going to believe this guys. What I'm going to tell you will blow your socks off. For real!' Ian was bouncing up and down in Mr Arturi's lab.

Zaf shook his head. 'Is this another of your stories – like the time you saw a bigfoot out in the bush?'

'Or the time you were sure you had found buried treasure,' laughed Tara.

'Ha, ha, ha. Nothing like that. This one's for real. I swear it is.'

'Give him a chance, you two,' Mr Arturi smiled.

'Don't ask me how or why,' Ian dropped his voice to an excited whisper, 'but I can control fire.'

'We all can,' chuckled Zaf. 'It's called matches. Is that it?'

'Not like that, you idiot. I mean, I can make fire happen from my body. I was out running round the track yesterday and whoosh! Flames shot out from my feet!'

At this Zaf and Tara burst out laughing. Even Mr Arturi was finding it hard not to join in.

'Ian, I know your feet stink, but this is the limit!' Zaf howled with laughter. Ian's face turned red.

'I'd listen to him if I were you,' a voice said from the doorway.

It was April. She closed the door and sat down.

'After what happened to me at the beach, I'd believe anything. Only I didn't have flames like Ian. I turned into water.' She saw the look on Zaf and Tara's faces. 'Yes, water.'

Mr Arturi took off his glasses and gave them a rub. It was one thing for Ian to come up with crazy stories, but April?

'Explain this to me,' he said, 'both of you. Start at the beginning and leave nothing out.'

***

Ian and April told their stories, describing just what had happened. The others had lots of questions. Zaf and Tara were no longer finding it funny. At the end, Mr Arturi cleaned his glasses again while he thought about what they had said.

'It must be something to do with the hydro-thermal explosion the other day,' he said at last. 'The impact. The gas you were exposed to is causing you to have hallucinations. Tricks of the mind. We ought to get all of you checked out by a doctor.'

'WE OUGHT TO GET YOU CHECKED OUT BY A **DOCTOR**.'

'This was no trick, Mr Arturi,' said April. 'I swear it was real.' Ian nodded.

'Hallucinations can feel very real,' said Mr Arturi. 'I'm taking you all to the hospital, right now.'

Ian had heard enough. He pushed his stool back and kicked off his shoes, then peeled off his socks, and stepped into the middle of the room. He closed his eyes, and concentrated.

Nothing happened.

'Ian...' said Mr Arturi. He sounded worried.

Ian's feet burst into flames.

The others yelped and jumped back. Mr Arturi dropped his glasses and stood up, jaw hanging open.

'Is this real enough for you?' Ian asked. He clicked his fingers and the flames were out. 'I already ruined two pairs of shoes,' he said, grinning. 'Mum is going to have a fit when she finds out.'

Mr Arturi was in a state of shock. He held on to his stool. If he didn't, he thought he might just fall off. 'You're right,' he said finally, 'that's no hallucination. I can't believe what I just saw.'

'Me neither,' muttered Zaf. He looked at where Ian had been standing. There was a burn mark on the floor.

'We need to find some answers and find them fast. I've got to go back to the mountain and take samples.'

Mr Arturi shook his head. 'There has got to be an explanation. In the meantime, *keep this to yourselves*. If word gets out about this, you'd become the biggest lab rats in the world.'

'Mr Arturi,' said Zaf slowly, 'if strange things have happened to both these guys, then it can only mean one thing…'

Tara nodded. 'That you and I are next in line.'

Chapter Five

Questions

After what had happened last time, Mr Arturi was leaving nothing to chance. Wearing a thermal radiation suit with a hood and breathing gear, he crept closer to the blast site. He kept his eyes glued to his meter.

He hadn't got much sleep the night before. In the end he had given up trying to lie in bed, and spent the night at his desk, checking and rechecking the information he had downloaded from the machines, trying to find some answers.

It had been no ordinary hydro-thermal blast. This had come from way down in the earth's crust. Almost like a major volcano going off. Somehow the eruption must have created a mixture of chemicals – the yellow gas he had found the kids choking on. Elements that had combined with the kids' DNA, unleashing some unknown energy force.

He had never known anything like it. How on earth did Ian create fire like that? And when April had taken them all to the pool, dived in and vanished into water, her swimsuit the only thing visible, Mr Arturi had practically fainted.

A line of wire had been strung up around the edge of the crater, stopping anyone from getting too close. Mr Arturi ducked under it. Wisps of steam leaked out of the hole in the ground. Inside the suit, Mr Arturi began to sweat.

Out of his back pack he took out a sample probe and hooked it up to a container. Then he snaked the probe down into the fissure, as far down as it would go. The container began to fill up. If any of that strange gas was still down there, maybe he could find out what was going on.

Before things got really out of hand.

Chapter Six

Earth

Tara came up with her own theory about what was going on.

It had nothing to do with science, or numbers. It had to do with dancing. Her parents' dancing, to be exact: that awkward, arm-jerking, feet-clomping, hand-clapping thing they did on the living room floor. (Tara was sure they only did it to embarrass her.)

There they were, after dinner, bopping about. She'd walked into the living room, covered her eyes and turned right back around. 'Hey, come and dance with us,' her dad had called after her. 'This is Earth, Wind and Fire – the best funk band ever!'

'Whatever,' Tara called back as she left the room. She had big things on her mind, not old-school 70s music. But something Dad had said rang a bell. Earth, wind and fire – she had heard that phrase before, and there was usually one more that went with that as well, wasn't there? Water.

Tara flipped open her laptop and quickly did a search. There it was: earth, wind, fire and water. The classical elements, the four things the Ancient Greeks thought everything in life was made up of.

Tara pushed away her computer, head spinning. Was the explosion the other day something to do with those elements?

Ian was obviously fire, and April was water, so that left earth and wind. Which one was she?

Tara wasn't going to sit around and wait for it to happen; she was going to find out right now. She crept down the hallway, past her sister's room, and out into the garden that backed onto the park. Her parents were still grooving away. She could hear the thump of the bass all the way at the bottom of the garden.

Right, she thought. *First up, let's try wind.*

Tara wasn't sure how to do this. She puffed out her cheeks and blew. Nothing. She closed her eyes and really concentrated. She imagined wind and hurricanes and gales. Still no dice. Then she flapped her arms and tried to make a breeze. Now she just looked plain ridiculous.

OK, so it wasn't wind. What about earth?

Tara dropped down on her knees and put her hands on the grass. She pushed the ground, hit it with her fists, tried to imagine herself as the ground. Zero. It wasn't working.

Maybe her theory was wrong. Nuts, even. Her parent's favourite band - what was she thinking?

Tara was annoyed. She picked up a clump of earth from the flower bed to chuck at the fence. And then it happened.

She felt a jolt in her hand and looked down. Tremors. The clump of earth was moving. Then her hand changed colour. It was the same colour as the earth.

The colour spread – right up her arm, like rivers of soil. Tara dropped the dirt in a hurry and clutched at her arm. She couldn't stop it!

But if she was honest, it felt good. Her whole body was changing into earth. She closed her eyes and felt it flood over her body, not fighting any more.

When she opened her eyes again, Tara gasped. She was a rich red, like the soil. Her arms, her legs – everything.

She shook her head. 'So, now what?' she asked out loud. 'You're the colour of dirt – big deal.'

She dropped to her knees again and put her hand on the lawn, and this time she felt a rush of power. The grass beneath her fingers began to grow. Fast. Right underneath her hand and through her fingers. She swept both her hands over the lawn like they were paint brushes. Now there were two streaks of long grass.

Tara grinned. This was cool.

'Now, that is very strange indeed,' a voice called out.

Tara jumped, and spun round, trying to cover up her arms. She couldn't see anyone.

'Who's there?' she called out.

HER **WHOLE BODY** WAS CHANGING INTO **EARTH!**

'I thought I was odd, but you really look like mud.'

It was Zaf. He was sitting on the roof of her house, a wicked smile on his face. He stood up, took a short run down the slope of the roof and jumped off the edge, arms wide.

And then he flew.

Chapter Seven

Wind

Zaf hit the ground and crumpled into a heap. He got up and dusted himself off. 'Still a bit clumsy,' he chuckled. 'It takes a little getting used to.' He looked Tara up and down and whistled. 'So you're earth, eh? I thought you would have to be.'

'You figured it out too? Earth, wind, fire and water. So what now? How long do you think we'll have these powers?' Tara asked.

'Search me. Days? Weeks?' Zaf paused. 'Forever?'

'Forever?' Tara whispered, shaking her head. 'That's a really long time.'

Zaf put his hand on her shoulder, and smiled. 'Might as well enjoy the ride while we can. Hey, watch this.' He turned and ran along the lawn, jumped into the air, and took off. Straight up. Using his arms like wings, he was able to swoop and dive, turn and bank. He hovered above Tara. 'It's like the air is carrying me.'

Tara watched in amazement. 'Pretty good, Zaf! Not too shabby at all!'

Zaf dropped to the ground. 'And I get the feeling that we're just touching the tip of the iceberg. I mean, who knows what we're capable of – look at the way you made that grass suddenly grow. I bet there's all sorts of nifty stuff you can do.'

Tara had to admit, he was right. 'Let's see.' She ran over to the rose bush, the one Mum could never get to grow properly, no matter how hard she tried. Tara touched one of the thorny branches and closed her eyes. All at once the bush sprang to life, shoots turned into more branches, then flowers began to appear. She stepped back. The rose bush was enormous – thick with flowers.

'Wow,' said Zaf. 'That is some power. Mind you, I'm not sure what your parents are going to think when they see all those roses in the morning.'

Tara gasped. 'That's right. I forgot. We need to keep this under wraps, don't we?'

Zaf laughed. 'Don't worry, they'll think it was just a freak of nature – what else could it be?'

Just then, from deep inside the park, came a squealing of tyres, the growl of a car engine, followed by a loud crash. It sounded like an accident. A big accident.

'Come on, let's go check it out!' said Zaf, jumping into the air.

Chapter Eight

Crash

Tara jumped over the garden fence and ran down the slope in the direction of the crash, trying hard to keep up with Zaf. The park was meant to be closed at night – so which fool had decided to race around in their car? Zaf darted through the trees, Tara panting behind him.

Down by the lake, they found what they were looking for. The car, or what was left of it, had ploughed straight into a tree. A total wreck. The front was a mess of twisted metal, the windscreen was shattered, and steam hissed from the engine. There was smoke in the air.

The tree was leaning at a dangerous angle, right over the car. It groaned and shuddered. It looked like it would collapse on top of the car. As if things weren't bad enough.

Zaf landed on his feet and scrambled down, while Tara caught up. He ran to the car window and leaned in. Both the driver and the passenger were slumped over, unconscious. Blood streamed from cuts on their faces. The driver had a trickle of blood coming from his nose. At least they were both still breathing.

Zaf tried to open the car door. It was jammed shut.

'It's no good, I can't reach them,' he yelled. 'But if we don't get them out, they're going to be crushed.'

'Don't move them!' gasped Tara. 'They could have neck injuries. We might make it worse.'

The tree groaned again. It snapped and jerked downwards. The trunk began to crack and splinter.

Tara took stock of the situation. 'I'll deal with the tree, try and get it to grow back – you go and get help. But don't let anyone see you flying!'

Zaf nodded. 'Will do.' He launched himself into the sky, and was gone in a flash.

Zaf shot over the tree tops, the air thundering in his ears. The best bet to find some police would be in the town centre.

Out of the park, he banked to the left and blasted along over the High Street, keeping himself high above the buildings and prying eyes. Within seconds he was in the town centre. How fast had he been flying? Fifty, sixty miles an hour?

He spotted a police car, down to his right, patrolling the street at a crawl.

Zaf flew over a darkened alleyway, braked to a halt, and lowered himself down almost like a helicopter. He hit the ground, and ran after the patrol car.

***

Back in the park, Tara had grabbed hold of the tree trunk, spreading her arms as wide as she could. She closed her eyes and tried to concentrate. She needed to stop the tree from flattening the car. Would this work?

Tara could feel strength surging through her arms, running through her veins, along her fingertips and into the bark. She could hear the leaves rustling, the branches shaking.

Slowly the tree began to rise, pulling itself away from the car. Tara gritted her teeth. The tree kept moving, bark crackling. At last it stopped.

Tara stepped away, heart pumping. The tree was upright.

There was a sound of sirens, getting closer. Tara looked down at her arms, which were still the colour of earth. She took a deep breath and focused, telling her body to change. How did you turn this thing off?

She tried to calm down, and as she watched, her arms slowly became lighter, and the earth seemed to sink back into her skin. The soil vanished.

Just in time. A police car roared down the footpath, lights flashing, and screeched to a halt. Zaf grinned at her from the back seat.

They had done it.

Chapter Nine

Answers

'You could have got hurt – and what if someone had seen you?' Mr Arturi paced up and down. They were in the science lab, gathered round a workbench, trying to get a handle on what was going on.

'But we didn't get hurt and no one saw our powers – I was able to change back,' said Tara.

'And the cops never saw me flying, I was careful,' added Zaf.

Mr Arturi sat back down, sighing. 'I guess you're right. But until we understand all of this, please try and keep it under wraps, OK? I don't want this to get out of control.'

'You mean I can't use my flames at the track and field competition next week?' Ian asked, chuckling. 'I was going to burn up the track – literally.'

Mr Arturi gave him a withering look. 'I think not.' He opened the folder in front of him. 'Hydro-chloride-magnesium-oxate,' he said, passing round a diagram. All he got was confused looks. 'The gas you inhaled,' he explained. 'From deep in the earth's crust. It's not a recognised compound. I can't find any research anywhere that mentions it.'

'Wicked,' Ian whistled looking at the diagram. 'Maybe we could bottle it and make a fortune. Want to fly like an eagle, or swim like a fish? Try our new hydro-chloro-watsit. Guaranteed results!'

'And this compound has transferred a sort of elemental energy into our bodies – and altered our genetic make-up. Is that what happened, Mr Arturi?' Zaf asked.

'That's my best guess,' said Mr Arturi. 'Though I don't know enough to explain how. And there's one other thing...' He sighed. 'I don't see any way the process can be reversed.'

'You mean we're always going to be this way?' said April

'I think you might.'

There was a silence around the table, as Mr Arturi's words sank in. Finally Tara spoke up. 'Well, I'm kind of glad.'

'Glad? How so?' asked April.

'Last night Zaf and I used our powers to do some good. Without us, those guys in the car crash might have died. I'd do it again.'

'You mean, like … be a superhero?' A smile was spreading across Ian's face. 'That I can handle.'

'Yeah, but what about the rest of the planet?' Zaf laughed.

Chapter Ten

Field Trip

The four of them agreed to keep things secret, even from their mums and dads. It would only scare the life out of them. But it was hard to go to about like normal when what they really wanted was to tear it up.

Mr Arturi told them they had to keep cool. The powers seemed to come on when they had a rush of adrenalin – like when April faced the shark, or Ian was pushing himself to run faster. If they didn't want to give the game away, they had to stay calm.

There were a couple of close calls. In the dining hall someone dropped their lunch tray by accident, and it landed on Zaf's lap. He jumped to his feet, soup all over his shorts, then took a deep breath and counted to ten. At the lockers, April heard someone making fun of her behind her back. She felt a crackle of energy flow through her chest, but just about managed to keep it in check.

Mr Arturi could see they needed to let off some steam or things were going to go haywire. It was time for another field trip – but this time without the explosions.

**

The van bounced down the dirt track, kicking up a cloud of dust. There was nothing but miles and miles of scrub in all directions. The early morning sun was already fierce. Up ahead they could spot some giant boulders reaching into the sky.

'Ugh, where are you taking us, Mr Arturi?' April groaned. 'This is the middle of nowhere.'

'See those boulders up ahead? I used to go there with my parents as a child.'

Tara raised her eyebrows. 'Your parents took you to see rocks? Nice.'

Mr Arturi laughed. 'They were geologists. What can I say, it kind of rubbed off on me. Besides, wait till you get there, it's more than just rocks.'

The track climbed a little now and the closer they got, the more the boulders towered over them. Some were like needles sticking out of the earth, others looked a little like archways, the rock worn smooth by the wind. They had to admit, it was pretty cool.

The van crunched to a halt and Mr Arturi switched off the engine. 'Welcome to Potter's Gully, your training ground for the day.'

'Training what, exactly?' asked Tara.

'What do you think? Your powers, of course. Come on, grab your packs.'

***

Mr Arturi led the way along a narrow path through the scrub. The path wound its way around some of the smaller rocks and into the shadows of the giants. 'By the way, don't stick your hands into any cracks or holes. Plenty of snakes about.'

'Great,' muttered Ian. 'First we nearly get blown up, now we have to deal with snakes.'

'Quit your moaning, superhero.' Tara shoved him in the back.

Mr Arturi clambered up onto a giant boulder, and climbed up the gentle slope to the top of it. It almost looked like there were steps carved into its surface. At the top, the group stopped, panting, to look at the view. It was some sight.

'Wow,' said April. 'You weren't wrong, Mr Arturi, this place rocks.'

Down below, in the middle of a circle of giant boulders, was a deep, blue watering hole surrounded by trees and plants. An oasis, completely hidden from the outside world.

'You see now why I brought you here? Earth, wind, fire and water. They're all here.'

'THIS PLACE ROCKS!'

Mr Arturi started sliding down the other side of the boulder. 'Who's for a swim? The water is deep and cool – trust me.'

It didn't take any persuading to get the four of them to dump their packs, rip off their shoes and jump in. April teased them by turning into water, flowing to the bottom and tugging at their legs.

'Quit that, will you!' shouted Tara. 'Wait till we're on dry land, and it's my turn.'

Chapter Eleven

Practice

After they had cooled off, Mr Arturi called them out to get started. They sat on the towels having a snack while he talked.

'If you're going to have these powers, you've got to learn to use them and control them wisely. It's just too dangerous otherwise. For you and for others.' He paused. 'Also, I think you've probably only scratched the surface as far as seeing what you can do. So today is about pushing yourselves. Go for it!'

'You heard the man, permission granted!' Ian jumped to his feet. He leaped over to the boulder next to the group and then ran, jumping from boulder to boulder, his feet blazing, as if they weren't even touching the ground.

Zaf climbed into the air, and chased after him, doing barrel rolls. 'Is that all you got?' he yelled after Ian.

'Typical boys,' said Tara, 'all that power, and all they want to do is play games.'

She climbed off the boulder and grasped the soil with her hands. Mr Arturi shook his head in wonder as he watched her body turn into earth. She flexed her arms, making them crackle.

'Lucky me, I guess I get to spend the day in the pool,' April said, smiling. She dived in, and came up in her water shape.

'See if you can breathe underwater, April,' Mr Arturi called out to her.

April nodded, 'OK, I'll give it a go.'

He turned to Tara. 'We know you can make things grow – let's see what else you can do.'

***

By the time Mr Arturi decided enough was enough, things had come a long way.

Not only was Zaf soaring through the air like he had been a bird all his life, he could push and pull the air with a wave of his arms. Spinning like a top, he made whirlwinds.

Fire had spread all over Ian, rising up from his feet, till you couldn't see him for flames. Then he discovered he could throw fire from his hands, and spent the rest of the morning blasting fireballs at the rocks, laughing his head off.

Mr Arturi had been right about April. In her water form, she found she was able to stay underwater as long

THINGS HAD COME A **LONG WAY**...

as she liked. More impressively, she could direct the water to her command: whirlpools, currents, waves, water spouts.

Tara could make the ground move – she was able to split the earth, and pull it back together again. She made mounds swell, and drop back down. She even got a small earthquake going, though she had to stop it pretty quickly when it looked like some of the boulders would start to roll.

And while all this was going on, Mr Arturi just sat and stared, his mind racing to try and figure it out.

'I can't believe this,' he said. 'Tell me I'm not dreaming.'

April sprayed a jet of water into his face. 'Awake now?' she said with a wide smile.

'Thanks a bunch,' said Mr Arturi, drying his glasses. 'Come on kids, it's time to get back.'

Chapter Twelve

Embers

While Mr Arturi's van rattled its way home, back in town two kids had decided to skip school. They were hanging out in Walcott Wood, bored out of their heads.

'Come on, we'll put it out before it gets too big – no worries,' the older of the two said, shaking a box of matches.

'I still don't reckon this is a good idea,' said the other. 'You saw the sign. Fire Danger Extreme, the arrow was pointing at. Why'd you want a fire anyway?'

The older kid shrugged. 'Dunno. Something to do. Call it survival training.'

He cleared a patch on the ground and started putting down stones in a circle.

'Look, we'll even put rocks down. Give me a hand.'

The younger boy shrugged his shoulders, and the two of them finished the fireplace, and then gathered up some twigs. It wasn't hard to find dry firewood, there hadn't been any real rain for months.

With a cheeky grin, the older boy struck a match and dropped it on the pile. It sat there for a moment, then the twigs caught and started to crackle.

The boys sat down to watch. The fire was really going now, and they had to shuffle back, away from the heat.

They watched for a few minutes, not saying anything. Their small pile of twigs burned down into glowing embers. The bigger boy got up to get some more wood.

'Nah,' said the other, 'I reckon that's enough.'

'OK,' chuckled the other, shaking his head. 'If you say so.' He sat down again.

The fire was almost burned out, but was still smoking. Now the older one scooped up a handful of dirt and threw it on the embers. The other boy did the same. Soon there was no more smoke.

'See, told you it wouldn't be a problem.'

'Yeah, I guess you're right.'

'You need to harden up. Come on, let's go.'

The two of them left the park.

But underneath the thin pile of dirt the embers were still hot. A gust of wind blew off the top layer of dust. Then another gust of wind caught a hot piece of ash, and carried it into the bush.

Chapter Thirteen

Action

Tara was back at home in her room listening to music. Just then, the news cut in on the radio. She turned it up:

'Local fire crews are battling to contain the forest fire – there are now reports of five separate fires – thought to have started somewhere in the vicinity of Walcott Wood. With such dry conditions, and with the wind picking up, containing the spread will be hard for the fire crews, and with every passing hour the blaze moves closer to town. The local fire department has called for additional assistance from three neighbouring counties. The sector commander is still uncertain as to the cause of the fire, though she is not ruling out arson.'

Tara flicked open her phone and called April. 'Have you heard the news?'

'I'm watching the TV now. Scary stuff. Looks like the fire crews are up against it. Think we could help?'

'You mean, like, use our powers?'

'Yeah – water and earth – might make a difference.'

'I'm in,' said Tara quickly, her heart thumping. 'I'll call the others. Let's meet at the back of the school hall to figure out what to do.'

'Great.'

It didn't take long for the four of them to get to the playing field behind the hall. Zaf and Ian hadn't needed asking twice and had raced over on their bikes as soon as Tara had called them. Zaf had brought a local map and had marked the spots where the fires had been reported. He had laid it out on the ground and was putting together a plan.

They would need to work fast.

'Tara, you head for the Green Lake up at the top here.' Zaf pointed at the map. 'See if you can form some sort of a ditch or gully leading from the lake to where the fires are.' He turned to April. 'As Tara makes the channel, you divert the water. As long as the water is flowing, you've got an escape route.'

'We're on it,' said April.

55

'What do I do?' Ian looked disappointed. 'I can control fire, but not one that big.'

'Ever hear of "back burning"?' asked Zaf. Ian shook his head. 'It's when fire fighters carefully burn a ring of bush so that the main fire can't spread.'

'I'm with you, kind of like a wall.' Ian's face brightened.

'But how are we going to do any of this without being discovered?' Tara asked. 'If we help fight this fire, our secret will be out.'

'I guess it's a price worth paying,' said April.

THEY WOULD NEED TO WORK **FAST**.

'Perhaps these will help,' said a voice behind them. The four students spun around.

It was Mr Arturi. He was holding some clothes. 'As soon as I heard the news I figured you would try to get involved, so I got three ski masks – they'll make it hard for you to be recognised.' He patted Ian on the back. 'No hard feelings, but I didn't think there was any point getting you one, it would last about a minute.'

He handed out three walkie-talkies. 'Use these radios to stay in touch. I'll be monitoring the emergency signal.'

Zaf quickly told Mr Arturi their plan.

'Sounds good,' he said. 'Remember, a fire needs three things to survive: fuel, heat and air. If you can cut out one of those things, you'll put it out. And Zaf, don't forget heat rises, so fly well clear of the flames.'

'Give me some credit, Mr Arturi, I'm well ahead of you.'

Mr Arturi nodded. 'April and Tara, I'll run you up to the lake in my van. Boys, bike in as close as you can before changing. Whatever happens, promise me: safety first.'

'What can happen?' Tara smiled. 'We're superheroes, right?'

'You said it.' Ian gave her a high-five.

'Then let's move,' said Zaf. He and Ian climbed on their bikes and sped towards the park.

'If we're going to keep doing this, we're going to need a smarter way of getting around,' grumbled Ian, pedalling hard.

Chapter Fourteen

Firestorm

Up in the hills, the fire was out of control. The flames ran like hungry beasts, clawing down the hillside towards town. The inferno was spreading fast. One minute trees were standing, the next they burst into fire, exploding like bombs.

Most of Walcott Wood had already gone – trees, bush, grass burnt to the ground. A smouldering heap of ash. In the middle of it somewhere, there was still a tiny circle of stones, the fireplace that couldn't hold the fire.

The roads leading up to the reserve were full of emergency teams. Hoses crisscrossed the tarmac like snakes. Fire crew from all over the area were fanning out across the hillside with shovels and equipment, fighting the fire on several flanks.

Up above, helicopters had started making water drops – the water plummeting down like giant cascades. But they hardly made a dent.

In the command bus, coordinating the battle, the sector commander stared at the map. She didn't like what she was seeing, or the reports she was getting over the radio. The water line from the lake still wasn't connected, the fire line wasn't being cleared fast enough, and they were running out of options. The town was in danger. It was time to send the call to evacuate.

But things were about to get worse.

Her radio crackled again. 'This is Delta 1, come in, Chief. Over.'

'This is command sector. Receiving. Over.'

'We're in serious trouble. Up on the ridge, two hundred metres from the summit. Fire's got right round us, Chief. We're getting squeezed. Going to try for the gorge. Over.'

'Drop your gear and get out now!' the chief shouted. 'Sending choppers to make runs your way. Over.'

'Understood. Over.'

The chief marked the map with Delta 1's position.

She bit her lip. Delta 1 were right in the middle of a firestorm, and unless the water bombs from the choppers could make a difference, there might be no way of getting them out.

***

Zaf and Ian tore along the road, legs pumping, heading out of town. 'I should have taken the flight!' Zaf panted.

Up ahead, a line of police cars blocked the road, turning traffic back.

'Looks like this is where we get off,' shouted Ian. 'Let's dump the bikes round the back of the bus station.'

The boys darted behind the building and skidded to a stop. They threw their bikes down.

Zaf pulled his mask over his face. All you could see were his eyes and mouth. That wasn't enough to hide his excitement.

'Find out where the fire crews are making their fire boundary – and follow their line. I'll make sure it blows in the right direction.' Zaf wagged a finger at his friend, 'And Ian, keep it under control, OK?'

'No sweat.'

Zaf jumped into the sky and shot up high, arms by his side. Ian closed his eyes and burst into flames. With a flash he was gone.

***

The fire crew down at the bottom of the hillside were racing to clear a line of bush, to give the fire nothing to feed on and nowhere to go.

But the gap between the fire teams and the blaze was getting smaller. They were running out of time.

The men and women working the line had seen a lot of fires in their time, they had battled many blazes, but what they saw next knocked them for six.

Along the fire line, sprinting hard, was a fiery figure. It was like the fire had come alive – a human fireball tearing through the bush. Its arms were pointed to the ground, hands blasting fire. Fire shot out from its feet, burning up a fire line. And the figure was laughing as it went.

The fire crews forgot what they were doing for a moment, and just stared.

Down swooped another figure, following in the fire-creature's trail. He was using his arms to throw

NOW THE FIRE FIGHTERS HAD SEEN **EVERYTHING**!

wind, fanning the flames, forcing them back towards the centre of the blaze, away from the fire crews. He blasted past like a jet.

Now the fire fighters had seen everything. First a human fire, like something out of a cartoon, and now some flying superhero wearing a mask.

The fire fighters cheered. Whoever they were, it didn't matter. They were saving the day.

Chapter Fifteen

Flood

Mr Arturi and the girls had headed out of town, and at the crossroads they doubled back and screeched along Lake Road, the old van whining as it pulled itself up the hills.

They had heard the chatter on the radio between the crew in trouble and the commander.

'We need to move fast, girls – I know a short cut.' Mr Arturi pulled the van off the road and they slammed onto a dirt track that led to the lake. They could see the fire trucks just down the shore, trying to rig up a water line. Within minutes the van reached the lake's edge, and skidded to a halt.

'Tara, direct your ditch along that ridge and head for the summit. The crew are just below, gravity will take care of the rest. April, jump in the lake and get that water moving, we need to get to those fire fighters now!' Mr Arturi grabbed his walkie talkie. 'I'm going to see where those boys are.'

***

The Delta 1 team were caught in a tiny pocket between the flames. Fire raged on all sides, and was closing in.

The choppers made another run, and water bombed down on the gorge, but it was below the crew's position. The choppers were trying to make them a corridor of escape, but the flames were too high for them to get in close and they kept missing their target.

Things were mounting up against the trapped crew. It was beginning to look like there was no way out.

Then from the summit above, barrelling over the ridge, came a flood of water as wide as a river.

The flood burst over the charred bush, exploding through the fire. Burnt trees fell to the ground and were smothered; flaming bush was doused. Smoke and steam

billowed into the air. Down the water cascaded, into the gorge, clearing a path.

'Come on!' yelled the crew leader. 'I don't know what just happened, but let's get out of here. Follow the water.' The fire fighters half clambered, half slipped down the muddy gorge, the fire still blazing on either side of them.

***

The line that Ian had burnt into the bushes was doing the trick – the main blaze had reached the line, and now had nothing to feed off. The fire crews had spread themselves out down the line, making sure it held. It looked like the town might just be safe.

Zaf landed by his mate's side. 'Ian, your job's done, better get out of here. Head near the road. I'll come and find you later.' He put his walkie talkie on the ground. 'Use this.'

Ian nodded. It was time to get out of sight. He killed his flames before grabbing the walkie talkie and ran down the hill, scrambling through the untouched part of the wood.

He found a clump of bushes, crouched behind it, and looked down at his body. There wasn't a scrap of clothing left. 'Great, now what?' he muttered. This clothes-burning thing was getting out of hand.

Zaf took to the air again. He began to circle the blaze, ripping around it like a jet, spinning the air back into the middle of the firestorm, whipping it into the centre.

'There's nowhere for you to run,' he growled at the fire. 'Just might as well give up now!' Round, and round he soared, forcing the fire back into itself.

As he flew past the lake below him, another tidal wave of water burst down the hillside, straight into the middle of the blaze, flooding everything in its path and doing the job faster than a hundred fire trucks could.

The fire was breaking up. *The fire crews can probably handle it from here*, Zaf thought.

He spotted Mr Arturi standing by his van at the far end of the lake, banked and flew down low, into the trees, hitting the ground running. Tara and April were already ahead of him.

'Good work, you three,' called Mr Arturi.

'You made it! We were getting worried,' April said, giving Zaf a hug. Her clothes were soaked.

'Nothing to it. I rode like the wind,' Zaf reassured her. 'We'll need to pick up Ian on the way out.'

'Let's go,' said Mr Arturi, 'before someone starts asking questions.'

The van spun round on the dirt track and raced towards the road.

Mr Arturi swung it onto the tarmac and headed back down the hill, driving carefully now, so they wouldn't attract attention. He slowed down as they neared the bottom of the hill.

'WHOA!' the walkie talkies all blurted. 'Slow down, I'm right here!' It was Ian.

Mr Arturi stopped the van.

The bushes to the side of the road shook and wobbled, and out from behind them struggled Ian. He had a leafy branch in front of him, and another branch covering his back, and he was totally naked, his face bright red.

'Don't say a word,' he muttered, as he climbed into the far back of the van. 'Not a single word.'

Chapter Sixteen

Hideout

'It is now believed that the fire crews have managed to completely contain yesterday's forest fire, having successfully created a fire break around the perimeter of the blaze. They are now patrolling the edge of the fire making sure it is extinguished.

'There are unconfirmed reports coming through of mysterious fire fighters using flame retardant suits and what appeared to be jet packs, and additional unofficial crew on the lake's edge using dynamite to re-direct the flow of water into the fire itself....'

Mr Arturi switched off the radio, and let out a long sigh as his shoulders slumped.

'That's a relief. I think I might just lie down now and have a heart attack.'

'But we didn't get into any trouble,' Zaf pointed out.

'Yeah, it was a piece of cake, Mr Arturi,' Tara insisted.

'I'd be up for doing it again,' Ian added.

'I'm with you,' said April. 'We could be heroes.'

They all looked at their teacher.

Mr Arturi thought for a moment. 'I suppose you really did do something wonderful up on that hillside. And now that I think about it, I haven't felt this good in a long time.' The others nodded at each other and broke into grins. 'But if you're going to do this hero thing, you're going to have to do it properly. No jumping in without looking first. OK?'

'Sure thing. We plan for every contingency,' said Zaf.

'First, we need to figure out a way to keep Ian's clothes on. Yesterday was ugggh.' Tara wrinkled her nose. Ian flicked her with a ruler. The others laughed.

Mr Arturi looked around the room. 'And I suppose we'll also need somewhere other than this lab to work from.'

'A hideout! A secret lair.' April's eyes widened. 'I like it.'

'And we'll need names,' added Ian. 'All the superheroes have them. How about I call myself Flash?'

'Already done – the Fantastic Four have a Flash,' said April.

'Yeah, but he was a comic book character, and I'm real.'

'Yeah, a real oaf,' Zaf laughed.

'I know, Ian,' Tara giggled, 'how about you call yourself Flaming Underpants.'

'Ha, ha. You two won't be laughing when I set fire to your school bags.'

Mr Arturi shook his head. 'What about Inferno? It means fierce fire.'

'Inferno,' whistled Ian, standing up and striking a pose. 'Now that I like.'

***

That week Mr Arturi found the perfect place for a hideout, a short drive out of town – the old airstrip. Back in the day it used to be an air force base. Only a few light planes used it now, but lying around the other side of the field away from the hangars were the hulks of abandoned jets. A plane graveyard, left there to slowly rust.

'RIG UP SOME POWER, A SMALL SCIENCE LAB, AND WE HAVE A **COMMAND CENTRE!**'

An old transport plane was set back further away than the others, at the edge of the field, close to some thick woods. By weaving a path through the trees Mr Arturi could get to the plane without being seen.

He managed to get the door open without too much trouble. The inside of the plane had been mostly stripped of anything that could be salvaged, but was still pretty solid.

Rig up some solar panels for power, a radio with an emergency frequency scanner, a couple of computers, a small science lab, and we have ourselves a command centre, Mr Arturi thought to himself.

When the others saw the place they were impressed. 'Wow, an old Hercules C-130,' Zaf marvelled. 'Good find, Mr Arturi, this place is the business.'

The going was slow. They could only work after school some days, and sneaking away over the weekend was hard without arousing too much suspicion. The four friends quickly got impatient.

April tried to reason with the others. 'If we're going to do this, we need to learn to lead double lives. Just remember to stay calm.'

Some days even she found getting through the school day, and sitting around the family dinner table almost too much to bear. But slowly the four of them learned to keep their eagerness under control, and keep their heads down. After all, there was no use being a superhero if you couldn't even get through high school.

Finally, the work on the plane was finished, and they were good to go.

Chapter Seventeen

Factor Four

'First order of business,' announced Mr Arturi with a wink. 'I've been working on some suits for you to use – if you're going to be superheroes you need to look the part.'

Mr Arturi showed them their outfits. Ian's was bright red, and made from flame retardant material – there'd be no more 'birthday suit' experiences. Zaf had a flight suit of blue, sleek and streamlined. Tara's was deep brown like the earth and highly flexible, and April had a silver wetsuit that would be barely visible in water. Mr Aruri had also rigged up masks from matching material with built-in earpieces and mikes.

'IF YOU'RE GOING TO BE **SUPERHEROES**, YOU NEED TO **LOOK** THE PART!'

'Now, what about the names you've been working on?' Mr Arturi asked once they'd all had a chance to try out their new suits. 'Ian's got Inferno. What about the rest of you?' He was enjoying this.

'I came up with Zephyr,' said Zaf. 'It's a type of breeze.'

'Nice,' smiled April. 'I'm going to call myself Aqua – Latin for water.'

'I found one that even sounds a bit like my real name,' Tara said. 'Terra Firma or just Terra for short. It means solid ground.'

Mr Arturi beamed. 'Couldn't have come up with better ones myself. Very catchy.'

'I've also had an idea about what we could call our group,' Zaf added. 'You know how there are four of us - what about Factor Four? Factor is like an element.'

'Has a ring to it,' Ian admitted. 'I like it.' The others agreed.

'Factor Four it is, then,' said Mr Arturi. 'Second order of business, what exactly do you want to do? How are you going to use your powers? I mean, we need to have a purpose. We can't just shoot from the hip.'

'Crime fighters?' suggested Zaf.

'Helping people?' April added.

'Rescuers, like we did the other day?' Ian shrugged his shoulders.

Tara was quiet for a bit. The others waited to hear what she had to say.

'I think there's a way we can do all of those things.' She hesitated. 'I have something to tell you, guys. After the fire, I waited a few days until it was definitely not smouldering anymore, and I went back to the hillside. And I made it all grow back again.'

'You did what?' Zaf exclaimed.

'The bushes, the trees, the whole thing. Go check it out. It's completely green again.'

'That's fantastic, Tara.' April gave her friend's shoulder a squeeze.

'But it got me thinking – we got these powers from deep within the earth, right? Well, maybe we're meant to use them to return the favour.'

'Like environmental activists?' Mr Arturi asked. 'I like the sound of that.'

'Yeah, I guess that's what I mean – only I was thinking more along the lines of eco-warriors. Cleaning up things, stopping environmental destruction, that kind of thing.'

The others thought about what Tara had just said. It made perfect sense.

The emergency radio in the plane buzzed to life, interrupting their thoughts. 'Mayday, mayday. This is oil tanker North Star in the channel just off the Godwin Rocks. Run aground. Repeat we've run aground. Oil starting to spill. Mayday.'

Mr Arturi looked at the group and whistled. 'Well, if that isn't a sign, then I don't know what is.'

The four got to their feet.

'Looks like it's time to get back to work,' said Zaf.

'Factor Four,' said Tara with a smile.

'Bringing you the power of earth, wind, fire and water,' declared April.

'About time too.' Ian clapped his hands together. 'I was beginning to get bored.'

Factor Four will return in
Tiger, Tiger